# The why and how of this book

Every month the Doctor Ann website (**www.teenagehealthfreak.org** and **www.doctorann.org**) receives over 1000 emails from young people asking questions about things that worry them about their body, their life, their health, their parents, and their friends. As well as lots of questions about sex and drugs, many young people write about their experiences of being bullied and ask how to deal with the bullies. This book contains some of these emails. There are questions on how to deal with friends, how not to become a bully yourself, how to cope when you are being bullied into having sex, as well as the nasty racist bullying that some young people have to deal with. What we have done is to pick out the most common problems, the most worrying ones and the ones that seem to make teenagers the most anxious, the most often – and to put them in this book along with carefully researched answers.

The website was originally set up because of the success of the books *Diary of a Teenage Health Freak* and *The Diary of the Other Health Freak*, both published by Oxford University Press in 2002. If you go onto the **www.teenagehealthfreak.org** website you can catch up with Pete Payne and all his worries about his spots, his girlfriend, his bicycle accidents etc in his day to day diary. Or you can read the books – whichever. And now you, like Pete Payne, can also find out what worries teenagers about bullying and how to get the absolute best answers – by reading this book.

D0194121

**AIDAN MACFARLANE** is a consultant paediatrician and public health doctor who ran the child and adolescent health services for Oxfordshire. He is now a freelance international consultant in teenage health.

**ANN McPHERSON** is a general practitioner with extensive experience of young people and their problems. She is also a lecturer in the Department of Primary Health Care at the University of Oxford.

As well as *The Diary of a Teenage Health Freak* and its sequel *The Diary of the Other Health Freak*, their other books include *Mum I Feel Funny* (which won the Times Education Supplement Information Book Award), *Me and My Mates*, *The Virgin Now Boarding*, and *Fresher Pressure*. They also published a book for parents about the teenage years called *Teenagers: the agony, the ecstasy, the answers*. Their most recent books are *Teenage Health Freak: Drugs* and *Sex*, which are in the same series as this book. The authors also run the extremely successful website on which this book is based – **www.teenagehealthfreak.org** – which receives around 250,000 hits a week and recently won the BUPA communication award.

### Authors' acknowledgements
We would like to thank: all the teenagers who emailed us – whether we were able to answer them or not – and all their parents for having them in the first place; Liz and the rest of the team at Baigent for their wonderful work on the website; Mike and Jane O'Regan for all their support and their funding; Ben Dupré for all his wonderful patience and 'suspect' sense of humour when helping us with the editing.

### Note
The answers we have given to the questions in this book are based on our personal clinical experiences as doctors when dealing with similar clinical problems. Young people reading the book will, we think, be helped by the answers that we have given. However, it is impossible for us to offer advice in such a way as to deal with all aspects of every individual's health problem. Therefore if you, as a reader of this book, have any continuing doubts or concerns about your health problem, we would strongly advise you to consult your own medical practitioner.

To preserve the true flavour of the originals, we have not changed or edited the language or spelling of the emailed questions used in this book. However, in the few cases where real names are used, these have been changed to protect the anonymity of the senders.

the truth

Bullying

# OXFORD
UNIVERSITY PRESS

Great Clarendon Street, Oxford OX2 6DP

Oxford University Press is a department of the University of Oxford.
It furthers the University's objective of excellence in research, scholarship,
and education by publishing worldwide in

Oxford New York

Auckland Bangkok Buenos Aires Cape Town Chennai
Dar es Salaam Delhi Hong Kong Istanbul Karachi Kolkata
Kuala Lumpur Madrid Melbourne Mexico City Mumbai Nairobi
São Paulo Shanghai Taipei Tokyo Toronto

Oxford is a registered trade mark of Oxford University Press
in the UK and in certain other countries

British Library Cataloguing in Publication Data available

ISBN 0-19-911230-4

3 5 7 9 10 8 6 4 2

Printed in Great Britain
by Cox & Wyman Ltd., Reading, Berkshire

# Contents

# All about bullying

It is difficult to know why we – young people and adults alike – have suddenly become so much more aware of bullying. We know that in our society physical violence is much less tolerated – with the abolition of caning in schools and the move to stop children being smacked, even by their parents. Although bullying has never really been acceptable, there has also never been a time when people have been so acutely sensitive to the need to stop it from happening.

One of the problems with bullying is that it takes so many different forms. Often, what is happening is obvious to both the person being bullied and to the person doing the bullying. But sometimes you may be unaware that you are being bullied but just know that you are being made to feel unhappy. Sometimes you may bully others without being sensitive enough to know that you are bullying. At other times your 'teasing' may overstep the mark and become bullying – it can be difficult to know where to draw the line. What we do know is that making other people's lives miserable by bullying should not be allowed to happen. What is also obvious is that most of us experience bullying at one time or another in our lives, and that many of us will also be bullies at one time or another.

By selecting from more than 50,000 emails that we have received from young people on the **www.teenagehealthfreak.org** website, we have been able to examine what bullying really is, how it makes young people feel, and how they deal with it themselves – both successfully and unsuccessfully. We have also been able to offer them advice on where to get help, and to put them in touch with recently available resources, such as the latest internet sites dealing with bullying.

# **BULLYING** QUESTIONNAIRE

**1**

**Do you think that you have ever been bullied?**
- ☐ 'Yes'
- ☐ 'No'

**2**

**If 'Yes' you do think that you have been bullied – who bullied you (you can tick more than one)?**

| | Yes | No |
|---|---|---|
| ■ One of your parents | ☐ Yes | ☐ No |
| ■ A brother or sister | ☐ Yes | ☐ No |
| ■ Some other pupil from your school | ☐ Yes | ☐ No |
| ■ A teacher at your school | ☐ Yes | ☐ No |
| ■ Somebody else | ☐ Yes | ☐ No |

**3**

**What have you been bullied about?**

| | Yes | No |
|---|---|---|
| ■ How you look | ☐ Yes | ☐ No |
| ■ Your height and weight | ☐ Yes | ☐ No |
| ■ Being a 'Groff' or 'Geek' (hard worker) | ☐ Yes | ☐ No |
| ■ Having sex | ☐ Yes | ☐ No |
| ■ Your race, colour or culture | ☐ Yes | ☐ No |

**4**

**How have you been bullied?**

| | Yes | No |
|---|---|---|
| ■ By calling you names | ☐ Yes | ☐ No |
| ■ By making you feel left out | ☐ Yes | ☐ No |
| ■ By threatening you | ☐ Yes | ☐ No |
| ■ By being violent to you | ☐ Yes | ☐ No |

**5**

**How did the bullying make you feel?**

| | Yes | No |
|---|---|---|
| ■ Frightened or scared | ☐ Yes | ☐ No |
| ■ Lonely and rejected | ☐ Yes | ☐ No |
| ■ Angry | ☐ Yes | ☐ No |
| ■ Violent | ☐ Yes | ☐ No |
| ■ Miserable and depressed | ☐ Yes | ☐ No |
| ■ Suicidal | ☐ Yes | ☐ No |

## 6 Which of the following do you think is bullying?

- 'A group of my "friends" are quite horrible to me and make me feel crap about myself and life.' ☐ Yes ☐ No
- 'No one likes me or wants to be my friend.' ☐ Yes ☐ No
- 'I am a girl aged 14 and this boy wants to sleep with me, and won't leave me alone.' ☐ Yes ☐ No
- 'No one will play with me at lunchtime – is it because I am black and they are all white?' ☐ Yes ☐ No
- 'My teacher says that unless I do better at maths he will put me down a class at school.' ☐ Yes ☐ No

## 7 What do you think you should do if you are being bullied at school?

- Take no notice and carry on as if nothing is happening ☐ Yes ☐ No
- Tell the person that is bullying you 'to get lost' or equivalent ☐ Yes ☐ No
- Hit the person who is bullying you if they are hurting you ☐ Yes ☐ No
- Tell one of your friends about it and gang up on the bully and 'get your own back' ☐ Yes ☐ No
- Tell someone you trust (teacher, parent, adult friend etc) about it and ask them to deal with it ☐ Yes ☐ No
- Get the person bullying you thrown out of school ☐ Yes ☐ No

(Note: There are no right or wrong answers to most of these questions.)

If you want to find out more about the issues raised by this questionnaire, read on!

# What is bullying?

It is unlikely that any of us will go through life without ever being bullied at all. But it is not always easy to know exactly what bullying is and why it is happening.

## ● THE WHAT, WHO AND WHY OF BULLYING

*Hi Doctor Ann.* **What is bullying?** 14 year old boy.

***Dear 'What is bullying?'*** — Bullying is when someone or several people do or say nasty or unpleasant things to you, or keep on teasing you in a way that you don't like. Almost everyone gets bullied by somebody at sometime in their lives. Sometimes it's hard to tell where teasing ends and bullying begins. Bad bullying is bad enough even if it just happens once, but it when it goes on and on it can become a serious problem.

*Dear Doc* — **Just how bad is bullying nowadays?** 13 year old girl.

*Dear 'How bad is bullying nowadays'* – This is a difficult question to answer. If you list all the things that might be called bullying like: hitting, biting, punching, pushing, spreading rumours about you, name-calling, trying to take your friends away from you – then there are very, very few young people who have not experienced these kinds of bullying at least once. If you are asking who has experienced these kinds of things regularly over quite a long period of time – say six months or so – then probably it is around one in five young people. I do hope that this has not been happening to you.

*Dr Ann* – **Why do people bully other people?** 13 year old boy.

*Dear 'Wanting to know why'* – People bully others for a whole range of different reasons. Some people don't feel good about themselves and they put other people 'down' in order to feel 'up'. To do this they may tease or taunt other people about lots of different things. These include: the way they look; the colour of their skin; how hard they work; if they have a physical or mental problem of some kind; if they come from another country; if they wear spectacles or have braces on their teeth. Bullies pick on almost anything, as long as they sense that they can make another person feel bad about themselves, or at least worse than the bully feels about himself or herself. Many bullies are people who were bullied themselves and the only way they can feel better is to do it to another person. Understanding this can be helpful to someone who is being bullied and might also stop them from becoming bullies themselves.

*Dear Doc* – **what do people with disability get teased for?** 12 year old girl.

*Dear 'What do people with disability get teased for'* – First, what is a 'disability'? It usually means some problem which makes you 'less able' and which can sometimes be a fairly minor problem or it can be a major problem like being paralysed and needing to be in a wheelchair. People who want to bully are always looking for a weakness of some kind in the person that they choose to bully; people with any kind of disability are an obvious target, because their disability is seen as a weakness which makes them particularly easy to pick on. Actually people with a disability are just normal people first and foremost with all the same feelings and needs as everyone else.

## ● BULLYING FOR NO REASON

*Ann* – **hi I was bullied a lot last year for no reason at all, it just all started one day.** I was getting really upset and did not tell anyone but it kept on going on. When I was being bullied I was kicked, punched, spat at and everything you could think of. I was even scared to come to school and walk home. Girl aged 14.

*Dear 'Bullied for no reason'* – I guess the reason these bullies were kicking and punching you was to look big themselves and seeing you scared made them feel powerful. Frequently bullies will try to make someone else miserable because it makes them feel better. It helps them with their own feelings of lack of confidence if they can see they can make someone else feel the same way. If you don't show any signs of giving in – then they usually give up (though they may go and find someone else to bully instead).

---

*Doctor Ann –* **why are people bullying me?** They make me feel shit about myself. 12 year old boy.

**Dear 'Why are people bullying me?'** – It is difficult to answer this without knowing you better. People usually tease and bully others because it makes them feel better. They may feel so miserable themselves that the only way that they can make themselves feel better is by seeing someone else (you) being more miserable than them.

---

*Dear Doctor Ann –* **I have a lot of problems** 1) boys keep picking on me 2) girls keep on using and abusing me 3) money problems 4) family problems 5) mum might have breast cancer. 13 year old girl.

**Dear 'Person with a lot of problems'** – It is a very sad fact of life that some bullies like picking on people who are 'down'. It sounds like your worries are piling up on you so it is time to talk. There are people who will want to help you. Try to find someone who will listen to how you feel sympathetically – someone from your family, a teacher, or maybe your family doctor.

# Different types
# 2 of bullying

People bully other people in many different ways. Some bullies hurt your feelings by calling you names or leaving you out of things. Other bullies actually hurt people physically.

● **NAME-CALLING**

*Dear Doctor Ann,* **I am being bullied by some people in my form at school.** They aren't hitting me, they're just calling me names and it really hurts. 14 year old girl.

*Dear 'Being bullied'* — There is an old saying: 'Sticks and stones may break my bones but names will never hurt me'. In fact I do not think the saying is true, as being called names is a really nasty form of bullying and often very difficult to deal with. Try to ignore the name-calling, though I realize this may be hard. Bullies get their pleasure from seeing that they are upsetting you. Link up with other friends so that you don't feel isolated. It does sound as though you are being made depressed by these bullies. Don't keep it all to yourself. Please tell your parents who can talk to your teachers. Some schools have special systems for dealing with bullies.

---

*Hi* – **I have been 'bullied' for nearly 3 years but I'm not sure if it is bullying because it doesn't happen all the time or by the same people.** I get called names, but only by some people. I have kept my feelings bottled up now for so long and I have only just started talking about it. I have no self-confidence  anymore or self-esteem. Is it depression? At school I'm talking to a counsellor though and I hope I'll feel better but I just don't know when!! 14 year old boy.

> ***Dear 'Being called names'*** – I think being called names is being bullied if it upsets you and even if it only happens once in a while. Although the name-calling may not be the actual cause of your lack of self-confidence it's not going to help. Unfortunately, when you are low on self-esteem, bullies sense this and pick on you. Being bullied then makes you feel more depressed and 'got at'. All these feelings together can be overwhelming, but good for you for doing something about it and telling your troubles to the counsellor at school. I am sure that you will start feeling better about it all soon.

## ● MAKING YOU FEEL LEFT OUT

*Doc* – **I hate getting bullied** – no one likes me or wants to be my friend. what am I doing wrong. What do I do to stop it? 13 year old boy.

*Dear 'I hate getting bullied'* – These feelings are true for us all, and sadly we almost all get bullied by someone at sometime in our lives, but that does not make it OK. You're probably not doing anything wrong yourself, but to stop being bullied there are a number of things you can try. First, don't give in to your bullies by showing that you mind. Secondly, relax about finding friends, but if you know someone else who is being bullied – start by making friends with them. Thirdly, tell an adult – a member of your family, a teacher, anyone you can trust – about what is happening and about how you feel about it.

---

*Dear Doctor Ann* – **I feel really left out of everything.** People do things and I don't know about them. I reckon its because no one likes me – even though I try and be friends with them. Boy 14.

*Dear 'Nobody likes me'* – Don't give up being nice to people yourself. Don't wait for other people to ask you to join in with them – take up a new sport or join a club for something you are interested in. This will boost your confidence and help you make friends. Then you will gradually find that other people will want to join in with you. It often seems that everyone is having a better time than you, but actually everyone, at one time or another feels a total lack of self-confidence. Perhaps if you try appearing more self-confident yourself, then other people will want to be with you.

---

*Dear Doctor Ann,* **a friend of mine is unhappy at school** as she feels that everyone rejects her. What should she do? Girl aged 14.

*Dear 'Person with a rejected friend'* — Unfortunately quite a lot of young people feel unhappy and rejected at one time or another. There can be many reasons for this and often it is several things that are going wrong that makes a person unhappy. Your friend may be feeling lonely or unsure of herself. She may be being bullied at school by friends, or be having problems at home. You may not be able to help her with some of the things that are making her unhappy, but just continuing to be her friend (even when she is not much fun to be with) will be important. If you are aware that she is being bullied then you could try to change this. You could suggest that you or she talk to the school nurse, her parents or another adult she trusts, to try to sort out the problem.

## ● THREATS AND VIOLENCE

*Dear A* — **a girl at school has been threatening me online saying that I will be beaten up by the end of the week** and when I go to secondary school. I thought it was just talk but today she started bumping into me and elbowing me when she walked by. My mom and I are having a meeting with the Head, but I don't think she'll do anything about it. Should I go to her mom or the police to have it on file? Please help me. My grades and family life are being affected by this. Thank you. 13 year old girl.

*Dear 'Threatened online'* — Threatening people using emails, mobile phones and text messages is just a new way of bullying. Schools are all meant to take notice of pupils being bullied – whatever way the bullying is being done. I would suggest that you try to get the school to take this up before involving the

17

police. Other practical things that you can do are – change your email address, block emails coming through from that particular person or from their mobile phone number. Remember to keep a copy of all the abusive emails so that you can really show people what has been happening – if you need to.

Dear Doctor Ann, **I have a bully at school, she hits me and kicks me then she says she's sorry,** then calls me names and steals my lunch, and then pretends she is sorry again. What can I do. Worried girl fan aged 14.

**Dear 'Worried and bullied fan'** – You should not have to put up with this from anybody. This bully obviously does not mean it when she says she is sorry. You do need to tell a teacher and your parents about this and they should stop it happening. Meanwhile try to avoid this bully and stick with your real friends.

Dear Doc – **help me please I am getting beaten up all the time at school and I have cuts and bruises on my face and legs** my mum keeps asking me where they come from and I just tell her I am clumsy but I don't think she believes me! What shall I do. 12 year old girl.

**Dear 'Getting beaten up all the time'** – I think that you actually know what to do. You need to tell your mother what is happening and ask her to contact the school to discuss the problem with your head teacher. Don't be afraid to do this – if you look at other people's experiences in this book you will see that this will make a big difference and should stop you being bullied.

# How Bullying

# 3 can make you feel

Lonely, rejected, scared, depressed or even suicidal – these are just some of the feelings that you can have if you are bullied. Sometimes you may feel sad and miserable and at other times bullying can make you so angry that you want to go out and bully other people. Below are some emails from people about the feelings they have when they are bullied.

## ● LONELY AND REJECTED

*Dear Ann* – **no one likes me they just ignore me what do I do.** How do I cope with being bullied? 14 year old girl.

> *Dear 'Everyone ignores me'* – It's miserable to feel that you are being ignored and that no one likes you. Sometimes it is truly happening and the people you want to be 'in with' just don't want to know. But sometimes it just feels like that because you are very shy, a bit depressed and find it difficult to join in unless people are very,

very nice to you. If it is this last reason, try talking to one person in the group who seems to be ignoring you and gradually you may feel more part of things. You will find others are feeling the same as you even though it doesn't look like it from the outside. Fortunately there are lots of different people in your class and I am sure you can start by finding someone to be friendly with, who will like you, and you can ignore those people who are bullying you.

---

*Dear Doctor* — **I hate being bullied.** It makes me feel lonely. Something needs to be done about it. Boy aged 13.

*Dear 'Hating being bullied'* — I am so sorry that you feel lonely. Everyone hates being bullied but the question here is what can you do about it? Have you tried talking to someone

about it – at school, at home, with friends, with other members of your family? Don't give in, and don't feel that you are alone with this, because there will be other people being bullied, and if you can find this person and stand up to your bullies together – you will be twice as strong – and much less lonely.

---

*Dear Doctor Ann,* **nobody likes me even though I am always nice to them – why is that? I am constantly being rejected from various social activities and it is really getting me down.** But I don't think they know how they are making me feel. Boy aged 15.

*Dear 'Feeling rejected'* — I am not surprised that you are feeling rejected if it is really true that nobody likes you. But I am sure that it just feels like that at the moment. Give up trying to get in with a crowd who for whatever reason don't want you – they are behaving like bullies and are not worth the trouble. Try joining in with other people who have some of the same interests as you do. And remember, even if other people seem part of the 'in crowd' they may not feel it inside. We all

feel outsiders and rejected at sometime in our lives, especially when we aren't feeling good about ourselves in other ways, or are depressed. But do talk to your parents or someone else you can trust about how you feel. Sharing the hurt often helps.

*Dear Ann* – **I cut myself recently because people called me names. I've been called the same name since year 5 and I'm now in year 9 which doesn't make it better and its really pissing me off.** One day I went home and cut myself until I really bled 'cos I love this boy who calls me names. Now this boy found out 'cos he asked my friend out and he calls me pathetic. 14 year old girl.

*Dear 'Called names'* – Cutting yourself may seem to help get rid of all your feelings of anger and anxiety in the short run, but it doesn't help deal with the real problem – which is you being called names. As it has been going on for so long – you definitely need to get help from other people. Start by talking with your friends and your parents, and involve your teachers too. When you feel like cutting yourself – don't do it. Try instead to make a list of alternative things to do and do one of them – phone a friend, go swimming, go for a run or go to the cinema. You deserve to spoil yourself not hurt yourself.

*Dear Dr Ann –* **I was beaten up 6 months ago now and I'm still scared to walk down the street on my own.** What should I do about it? 13 year old girl.

*Dear 'Beaten-up' person –* It is time to get your self-confidence back. You'll need to do this gradually. I guess you are happy to walk down the street with a friend, so why not try walking some of the way on your own, and then go further and further each day until you can do it all on your own without worrying. Don't hang around feeling scared – take your life back again for yourself.

*Dr –* **I'm really scared I was wiv my m8s n dis grl came up strtd mouthin off n punchd 2 ov em i fink i wil b nxt n im scared 1 of d grls in d grup goes 2 our skul she as dun nuffin.** d police were involved bt im stil scared bout goin out. 13 year old girl.

*Dear 'Scared' –* Don't let a couple of mean, useless, pathetic bullies make your life a misery. You and your friends need to stand up to them together – or tell someone else about them. You could also consider doing judo for self defence and then you might feel more confident that you can handle any physical bullying in the future.

*Dr –* **I keep on getting bullied and I don't know what to do I am too scared to fight back and I told my mum and she said fight back.** Can you help me. 14 year old girl.

*Dear 'Being bullied'* — There are many ways of fighting back. The best one is learning how to ignore your bullies. Don't respond to them calling you names or pushing you or doing anything to you. Keep out of their way. Bullies feed off the responses of their victims. If you don't respond they should leave you alone and you can stop feeling scared.

---

*Hi Dr Ann* — **I am 15 and am worried about going out with my mates on a Saturday night because this guy (18) says he will beat me shitless**. I really need help to make me feel easier about going out with my mates. 15 year old boy.

*Dear 'Worried about going out with my mates'* — You have mates and mates are there to help you. Talk to them about what is happening. To ask for help is a sign of strength, not weakness. If you talk to your friends about your feelings, then they will hopefully talk to you about theirs. There may be others amongst your friends who are being bullied by this same guy, so team up and show that if he wants to stay mates he has to accept all of you together.

## ● DEPRESSED

*Doctor Ann,* **I am really depressed.** I am being bullied at school and am being called names like 'freak', 'geek', 'boffin' and a long list of other unsuitable names. I am going out with this boy and all the boys like him as he gets himself in trouble but all my mates think I am mad and to them I am classed as a loser. I have tried talking to them about it but they tell me to get a life. Should I dump the boy for my friends or keep the boy and tell them if I had to pick between them and him I'd pick him. Help please! 12 year old girl.

*Dear 'Absolutely not a loser'* – Sounds to me as if your friends may be worried about you going out with the wrong bloke or it could be that they are envious of you. Don't necessarily give in to them but do think about what they are saying. Stick with your boyfriend if you decide that is the right thing. Your friends will respect you if you show them that you have a mind and will of your own and won't let them dictate your life. But – are you really sure that being with this boy is good for you?

---

*Dear Ann* – **I have moved school because I was getting bullied, I got really down and even tried cutting my self because of it and tried being sick.** Please help me before I do something bad. Girl aged 13.

*Dear 'Really down'* – You need to get help straight away. You shouldn't be managing this on your own. Your first step should be to tell your parents or school nurse and get them to arrange for you to see your doctor. He/she will help you.

---

*Doc* – **I have been bullied since I was five I am a fat ugly 15 year old now and do not think highly of myself.** 15 year old girl.

*Dear 'Bullied since the age of five'* – I am so sorry that you have had your self-confidence damaged in this way. It sounds as if you have been made to feel so badly about yourself by the bullies (even if they have stopped now) – that you see yourself as fat and ugly, even if you're not. I think that you need to go and get expert help. The best person to start with would be your own family doctor who will hopefully refer you on to a psychologist. Going to see a psychologist doesn't mean you are going mad or anything. If you have a headache you take pills to make it go away. Seeing a psychologist is just like taking a pill – it's a way of helping you get your self-confidence back to make you feel better.

---

*Dear Ann* – **I was bullied by year 9 people when I was only 11 years of age they broke my leg and kicked me in the ribs several times I will never forget that time.** Boy aged 16.

*Dear 'Never forgetting'* – I hope that people who bully read this so that they know what effect they can have on people's lives even many years later. It might help you get over this tough time in your life if you talk through your feelings with someone like a counsellor or a psychologist. Have you tried this?

## ● SUICIDAL

*Dear Dr Ann.* **I need some help.** I am lonely in the world and nobody loves me because I have a lot of spots and my last girlfriend said my willy was too small. Everyone thinks I am a geek and it is going round that I am gay. What should I do? I really want to leave school and I have been thinking of suicide. PLEASE HELP ME! 17 year old boy.

*Dear 'Suicide thinker'* – I think that you need help from someone very quickly. The question is who would you find it easiest to talk to about this? Have you tried talking about the way that you feel with someone that you trust and who is close to you – your parents, a teacher or a doctor? Don't bottle these feelings up inside you – talk to other people about them. Think positive! First deal with the spots – your doctor can give you some medicine for them – so that is one thing out of the way. Next – at least you have had a girlfriend (even if she was mean). Try to ignore the negative comments from others. Listen to, and think about, the positive things about yourself.

---

*Dear Doctor Ann –* **my problem is that when my periods are due I feel like dying because the bullies pick on me more at this time of the month and I don't know why.** 15 year old girl.

*Dear 'Bullied monthly' –* Some women feel more vulnerable and sensitive around the time of their periods and I think this is happening to you. The bullies are probably picking on you at other times in the month too, but maybe it doesn't get to you so much then. Try keeping a diary to see if it is just 'that time of the month' that is making you feel so upset. If it is – then try staying away from those who are bullying you when you are feeling vulnerable. If that doesn't work then you should consider telling someone about those who are bullying you.

---

*Dear Doc,* **I am being bullied and my teachers are not helping me.** I am unhappy all the time and the last time I cried about it they sent me to a psychiatrist. I can't take this for much longer. 15 year old girl.

> **Dear 'Unhappy all the time'** – It sounds as if you have been made to feel very unhappy over a long period of time by the people who are bullying you. It seems like your teachers just don't realize how bad things still are. It's time to take further action now – before things get worse. However difficult it is, you need to tell the psychiatrist that you are seeing that something must be changed at your school to help you. If you are finding it difficult to talk to the teachers at your school – get your psychiatrist to do it for you, or at least 'with' you.

*Dear Doctor* – **I really want to kill myself at times.** People make fun of me and laugh and I want to make a statement to let people know they are hurting me. The only one I can think of is ending it all can you help. 15 year old boy.

> **Dear 'Wanting to kill yourself'** – YOU NEED TO GET HELP NOW BY TELLING SOMEONE ABOUT HOW YOU FEEL. This is a much better way of making a statement to the bullies than hurting yourself. What it will do is help ensure that the bullies stop bullying you and hopefully bullying others as well. Hurting yourself won't hurt your bullies – they will just know that they have succeeded in getting at you.

# Who
## 4 bullies?

A great deal of bullying is done by people who the victims know quite well – so-called 'friends' or others who play a part in their daily lives. Sometimes this bullying is deliberate but at other times it may be teasing that has gone too far. Either way it can still have the same effect on the person at the receiving end!

● **FRIENDS?**

*Dear Doctor Ann* – **my friends beat me up all the time and they still do it.** There is nothing I can do about it. They are horrible friends but they are my best friends. 14 year old boy.

*Dear 'Nothing I can do about it'* – No, no, no – don't accept that. You are worth more – far, far more. There are lots of people out there who will be your friend if you give them a chance. You've got to tell these people they can only be your friends if they treat you properly. Tell them that if they go on beating you up you'll go and find friends who are not mean, petty bullies like they are.

*Dear Ann* – **I am being bullied by my ex best friend what shall I do?** Girl. Aged 16.

*Dear 'Being bullied by ex best friend'* – Maybe your ex-best friend is bullying you because you dumped her and made her feel bad about herself? Maybe you've made her feel jealous and rejected because you have made new friends and she feels excluded from your group? This doesn't excuse her behaviour, but may explain it. Why don't you try talking to her about this?

---

*Hi Dr Ann* – **I was being bullied by my best friend at school.** She used to call me horrible names and leave me out of things. She tries to cheat off me in tests but I try and not let her. One day she pushed the biggest girl in my class into me and I hurt my arm. Another time she pushed the same girl into me and winded me. She never said sorry. I hang around in a group of 4-5 people. Sometimes when she calls me names they just laugh. I am friends with the other people in my group and they all are friends with the

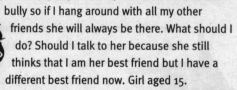

bully so if I hang around with all my other friends she will always be there. What should I do? Should I talk to her because she still thinks that I am her best friend but I have a different best friend now. Girl aged 15.

*Dear 'Bullied by best friend'* – What you tell me here shows how complex human relationships and friendships really are and you are learning fast. You have this 'best friend' who shows off in front of your other friends by bullying you because it makes her feel powerful (which she probably needs to feel because she actually feels weak most of the time). You are probably afraid of losing them all as friends if you stand up for yourself... but you won't. Try it and see – talk to this 'not best friend' and say that you won't take any more of her bullying and explain the way it makes you feel.

---

*Doctor –* **I am getting bullied a lot I can't put up with it anymore and the whole class, even my friends, are ganging up on me.** 17 year old girl.

*Dear 'Picked on by the whole class'* – It may feel like the whole class is against you but I am sure that there is at least one person not ganging up on you. It is time to get help now. Tell your teacher or the head teacher and let them sort it out. Don't be ashamed to do this – you are probably not the only person having problems like this so you'll be helping others too. If it doesn't get better maybe the only solution is to change classes.

---

*Dear Dr. Ann,* **I play football and the rest of the team bully and beat me up and say that I let the side down, but I want to be mates with them.** There seems to be nothing I can do about it because I like being with them but they are horrid to me. 14 year old boy.

*Dear 'Person with horrid football mates'* – You can and must do something about it. Tell someone about this (the coach?) to stop them beating you up. In the end they are likely to respect you more. It is stupid of them, because if there is one member of their team who is made to feel awful then the team won't play so well together. Can you find a new team to play with?

---

*Doc* – **a group of my 'friends' are quite horrible to me and make me feel crap about myself and life and make me want to die.** Should I leave the group and make new friends? I've considered this before but am scared they will be really nasty to me if I do. 15 year old girl.

**Dear 'Person with horrid friends'** – Yes, dump these so-called 'friends' now. You don't need them if they are making you feel like crap. Don't be scared, be positive and self-confident and think about the fact that there will be many, many people who want to be your friend because you have so much to offer. There will be genuine friends out there who make you feel good about yourself – go find them.

---

*Dear Doc* – **I am bullied by my friends and I don't think they like me, I follow them round and buy them things but they still enjoy hurting and taunting me.** What should I do as they are my only friends? Boy aged 15.

**Dear 'Being bullied by friends'** – These are not 'friends' – they are bullies and they seem to enjoy bullying you. Don't give in to this. There are going to be many, many people who will want to be your friends and who won't treat you badly and don't need bribing. Friends should be there to help and appreciate you, not to hurt you. Keep looking and you will find people who enjoy doing things for other people – like looking after them and supporting them at bad times.

*Doctor* my 'friends' keep on taunting me, abusing me, imitating me, pushing me and running away from me at lunchtime and I come home miserable and unhappy but it is still going on. What do I do? Girl aged 13.

> *Dear 'Made to feel miserable and unhappy by friends'* — People (whether friends or not) who persistently bully are often people who have been bullied themselves, or lack self-confidence. It makes these people feel good to exert power over other people. But they know what they are doing, as they run away like cowards. Ask an adult you trust to help – you shouldn't be dealing with this alone.

● **OLDER AND SHOULD KNOW BETTER**

*Dear Doctor Ann* **I am being bullied by a boy 6 years older than me.** It is really nasty because they pick on me in front of a few people and it's only me because I'm the smallest. They are 18 and I am 12. It really upsets me. Boy aged 12.

> *Dear 'Being bullied by someone much older'* — Bullies often pick on someone much younger. Most bullies want to make themselves feel big and powerful. So they pick on people who are at a disadvantage – someone much younger or someone with a disability or someone from a minority group racially or culturally. In a way this is what makes bullies so pathetic – that they themselves feel so weak that they have to pick on the even more vulnerable. My advice to you is to stay away from this boy and his group. You may be small but be big inside.

*Dear Ann* **I am writing to you as a first. I have recently been bothered by this older boy and he brings his friends around wherever he goes.**  Recently I was coming from school to my friend's house when he came over to me and said what have I been saying about him and I said nothing. I don't even know the boy too well so why would I talk about him. He hit me a few times and my friend was gonna fight him but he head butted me and my friend + also he picks up weapons to fight people. He is known for fighting people and likes it. He now lives near my house and I am scared to even go to the shop. I have seen him a few times around here but when I see him I hide from him. What should I do p.s I have told my Dad.

> *Dear 'Picked on by an older boy'* – You have made a good start by telling your Dad, and I hope that he (your dad) is being supportive of you. It sounds as though this boy just picks people at random to bully and sees if they can be terrorized by him because that is the effect that he is looking for. Don't give in to it – as a starter, get your Dad to go around to the shop with you. It might help if your Dad talks to him and tells him that if he ever threatens you again then he will involve the police. Boys like this bully don't want to be hassled themselves, so he will probably back off immediately if he is challenged.

# 5 Can families bully?

Teasing in families happens all the time and can be a sign of affection. You have to know someone quite well in order to tease them. But sometimes teasing goes over the top and someone gets hurt and upset. A person who takes a tease quite happily one day, may be totally hurt by it the next. It very much depends on the situation.

## ● BROTHERS AND SISTERS

*Dear Doc* — **I am very worried about my older brother.** He gets shredded very easily and 2 days ago he hit me in my face and nearly blinded me. I am now really scared that next time he might really hurt me. Please help me. 12 year old girl.

*Dear 'Worried about your brother'* — You might be surprised to know that bullying between brothers and sisters happens quite a lot. You need to talk to your brother and tell him that what he has done is not on and that if he does it again you will tell your parents about it. Keep to this promise – your parents should have zero tolerance towards this kind of violence. 'Zero tolerance' means that absolutely all bullying is dealt with immediately there and then, and no allowances are made in letting off the person doing the bullying.

*Dear Doc* – **my brother is 15 and lately he has been spending nearly 3 hours on the computer each night playing games.** Whenever I try and tell him to let me have a go he swears at me and threatens to hurt me. But 2 days ago he actually punched me just below my eyebrow (nearly my eye) and now I am really scared he might do it again or something even worse. He says he'll kill me if I go to mum about it. Please help. 14 year old girl.

*Dear 'Brother punched me'* – Don't take any notice of your brother's threats. Your brother has to learn to share the computer with you. You could drive a bargain with him – you won't go to your mum, if he lets you have more time on the computer. Negotiate and compromise – that's what life is all about. If the problem continues or he hits you again, you should tell your mother about it straight away.

● **PARENTS**

*Dear Doctor Ann* – **My mum and dad split up and every since I've lived with dad. The thing is he's started to beat me up and things.** I don't know what to do, as he hits me with anything and everything. I need your help as he doesn't stop. I hate him. My brother is 16 and he doesn't know about it. Should I tell him? I am aged 13.

> **Dear 'I hate my dad'** – Yes, tell your brother and ask him to get help for you. Otherwise tell your mum, if you are still seeing her, or anyone else that you trust, such as another family member, a teacher, neighbour or doctor. Finally, you could try ringing the free Childline on 0800 1111. Talk to them about it or try their website www.childline.org.uk. Take care.

*Dear Doctor Ann,* **my parents keep fighting and yesterday my mum got a black eye but she said she fell down the stairs.** What can I do, I just want the violence to end!!! Girl aged 14.

> **Dear 'Daughter whose parents fight'** – This is a terrible reminder that adults bully each other as well. Unfortunately violence in the home, especially men hitting women, is all too common. It is usually hidden because the people to whom it happens are too embarrassed to admit what has happened and cover up like your mum has. The victims often blame themselves for the violence. But it is absolutely wrong. Try talking to your mum and don't be afraid to tell another adult you trust, as keeping it all to yourself makes it even worse.

# Why people get bullied – school work

When you're a teenager you spend half your life at school and it is one of the commonest places for getting bullied. Bullying at school can be for many different reasons. Other students cause most of the bullying that happens in schools, but occasionally teachers can be bullies too.

● **BEING GOOD AT WORK**

*Dr Ann* – **I was bullied in school because I always done my work and they used to make me cry.** Every one called me a cry baby but when I told my mum she made me go and tell the head teacher and she made it stop. Girl aged 13.

*Dear 'Person being bullied for doing their work'* – The people who bullied you were probably just envious of you for doing well so they wanted to make you suffer too. You seem to have dealt with this very sensibly by yourself – well done – it shows that if you tell someone about being bullied you can get it stopped.

---

*Dear Doctor* – **I'm at a secondary school in Surrey. I'm bullied because some people (teachers, friends, other pupils, etc) may class me as smart.** People bully me because of this. Boy aged 13.

> ***Dear 'Person who is smart'*** – Stay smart and ignore the bullies. Don't take any notice of them and they will find something else to do. Bullies need to be taken notice of. They like people to react and if they do – they keep on bullying. So don't react – keep on working and they will give it up.

---

*Doctor Ann,* **I had a very bad bullying problem.** I had been getting bullied by boys and girls who were older and younger than me (I'm 14). A boy had come up and punched me at break time. 1 of my friends told my French teacher. I was shaking so badly from shock. The boy who had punched me got put on a personal report. I never told my mum or dad. They bullied me because I was good at work in school and that I didn't do all the boyish things like football. I told my year head + headmistress. Tell someone and don't be scared I reckon. Bullied victim boy aged 16.

> ***Dear 'Winner'*** – You are absolutely right. That's excellent advice – tell someone and show that you don't mind.

*Dear Doctor,* **I really enjoy working at school but people call me a groff, so I have started pretending not to work.** But the teachers are getting at me because I've decided the best way is not handing in my home work but I'm worried that they'll do me down in my course work. Boy aged 15.

*Dear 'Worried about your work'* – The long-term losers here are those who don't see that working hard now means doing better in life later on. So don't let the bullies get to you. You don't want to end up in some boring job like they will! Hand that course work in.

## • LIKING DIFFERENT THINGS

*Dear Doctor Ann* **I think I am totally different from everyone else at school and listen to classical music and play an oboe at grade 8!** Everyone teases me for this. Is there some way i can boost my self-confidence? 15 year old girl.

*Dear 'Oboe player'* – Hang in there and stick with the oboe playing. Your friends may tease you now but you will be in huge demand in the near future as the world and orchestras are desperately short of good oboe players. Also there are lots of brilliant guys around in orchestras who, like you, are into the classical stuff.

## HAVING WORK PROBLEMS

*Dear Dr Ann* — **I have a real problem reading out loud in school.** Whenever I'm asked, my heart starts beating really quickly and I get out of breath and I struggle to talk. The last few times I've had to pretend to feel ill so I can go outside to get some air.

This is really embarrassing for me and I get bullied about it. This is just a recent thing that has started happening, it didn't used to happen to me at all. Please help!

*Dear 'Problem reader'* — **Sounds to me as if you are getting panic attacks.** A 'panic attack' is like feeling very frightened about something that you shouldn't need to feel frightened about. What happens when you get an attack is that your body releases a hormone called adrenaline, which makes you breathe fast and your heart race fast.

The best way to help yourself is to start reading out loud at home to your parents, and then do it in front of a teacher alone (after explaining your problem to the teacher). Then try doing it in front of some friends. This gradual approach should mean you can read out loud without getting panic attacks, and stop you from being bullied both at the same time!

## MESSING AROUND

*Dear Dr* — **sometimes I get picked on by teachers because they say I mess around in class, but I don't , and I can't take it any more.** Girl aged 14.

*Dear 'Being picked on by teachers'* — Yes, teachers can be bullies too, though only you will know if what they say is true or not. Have a long hard think about this. If you really feel that you are being unjustly accused then you are going to have to tell someone you trust about the way that you feel, such as one of the teachers who doesn't bully you, or your parents. Teachers can be very sarcastic sometimes and make you feel small in front of others, which can be another form of bullying. Schools are all meant to have policies to deal with bullies amongst their pupils but they sometimes forget about bullying by teachers. Don't 'do nothing about it'. If you are feeling bullied by the teachers, there must be other pupils who feel like you do and you owe it to yourself and them to do something about it. Speak out now.

# Why people get bullied - for being different

'Being different' is another reason people get bullied. Many people follow fashions and try not to stand out too much. Others choose to dress or look differently as a sign of their individuality. Some people look or act slightly differently to others because that is simply the way they are. Many of the most successful people in the world have had the self-confidence to carve their own path and stand up for what they believe in – and this might be you!

## ● STANDING OUT FROM THE CROWD

*Dear Dr. Ann* **I get bullied because I look different to every one else so every one picks on me including the teachers at school.** What do I do? 15 year old girl.

*Dear 'Person who looks different and gets picked on'* – Here are two ideas for ways of dealing with this problem from other people who have been bullied. Joe suggests: 'Stand up to the bullies. Don't walk past them with your head down and a grim face. Walk past, holding your head up high and smiling, and be confident. Show them they don't hurt you (even if they do). Don't lower yourself to their

level, if they call you names don't get mad or call them back just laugh it off and walk away – show them they don't bother you.' Liddy says 'I am being bullied at the moment. I usually twist their words round to go against them or turn what they say into a compliment. It works. For instance, if they said "You're a geek", I'll say, "I'm a geek and proud of it!" They can't really say anything back to that in my experience!'

---

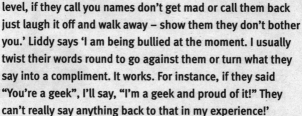

*Dear Doc –* **I am getting a lot of crap for being a Goth.** Because I live in a small town minds are very closed and the attitude to me seems to be 'satanist slut'. I tried being nice. Tried explaining that it was just a way of dressing, not a weird cult or anything. But I still have to put up with insults and the occasional hand up my skirt/ threat of rape/ person trying to perform surgery on me with wire cutters. People think I can handle it but I really can't, especially not when I have to go back to school, especially as I have just had a close friend die. I'm scared I'm going to really hurt the next person who says 'so who died?' or 'devils

daughter' or anything else to me. I don't like hurting people though. I've only snapped ONCE and I nearly killed the boy who said the things. Can you help stop me really hurting someone who although they might deserve it is probably quite nice to everyone else? 15 year old girl.

---

*Dear 'Taking crap for being a Goth'* – The trouble you are facing is common to anyone who the general population considers 'different' in any way. It doesn't really matter if it's because someone is taller or shorter, cleverer or more stupid, have more hair or less hair etc than Mr or Miss Average, some people are always seeking some excuse to vent their own hang-ups on other people. But knowing that almost everyone gets bullied/teased for something is not going to help you. You have decided to do your own thing and that is great – but your statement about being a Goth does threaten other people who would prefer you to be like them. In deciding to be different you also need to be strong about sticking with it and not caving in to the ordinary! What you need is sound advice and you won't get any sounder than the advice given in chapters 13 and 14 from people who have been through it themselves. Check it out, because the main messages are – don't show that you mind the bullying and, most of all don't go bullying other people because they bully you.

## BEING FANCIABLE

*Dr Ann* – **I was bullied because people think I am a slag because a lot of people fancy me and I have had quite a few boyfriends.** But they don't get it that you are only a slag if you sleep with a lot of people – which I haven't. In fact I haven't slept with anybody. But I still need advice and help about what to do. When it happens I normally get hit at school and it ends up as a fight but I can't just stand there and do nothing. So I

44

fight back but because people crowd around you shouting 'FIGHT' I lose all my confidence and go all weak. I normally end up losing the fight and get people coming passed me saying 'Haha, you got banged'. Most people  pick a fight with you because they think you're a soft and easy target. The thing is though, if you don't lose the fight then the person who you won the fight against will get someone bigger and harder to beat you up. I don't think that is fair. People should fight for their own battles. 15 year old girl.

*Dear 'Fighter back'* – What the bullies want from you is a reaction. They want to know that they can get at you – and they know this because you fight them. You show that you are hurt by fighting back. I absolutely agree that 'people should fight their own battles', but the best way to win this fight is by

 using a weapon that your enemies can't compete with – indifference. This is not being 'soft' or 'easy'. If you ignore the bullies you take away their reason for taunting you. Without a reaction, they should get tired of playing this game and leave you alone.

● **NOT 'FITTING IN'**

*Dear Doc,* **I am 13 and at school I don't really fit in with the boys so I hang around with the girls more.** I think by doing this I may be a bit more feminine than the other boys. That may be true, but most of them call me gay and a poof. I am not. I really am not gay. Although I don't really show it, this is really getting me down and I am starting to

wish I could fit in with the boys I have tried to hang with them but they just ignore me or tell me to go away in different words. 13 year old boy.

*Dear 'Being a bit more feminine'* — Being a woman myself I don't see anything wrong with a man being a bit 'more feminine' – actually rather a good thing. Calling people 'gay' or 'a poof' is a favourite amongst bullies – maybe because they have a sneaky feeling that this might apply to themselves. There is nothing wrong in being either 'feminine' or homosexual. Chances are the boys are jealous of you because you get on so well with girls.

*Dear Ann* — **I feel that I'll never have a friend who I can really talk to. I'm classed as a 'greebo' 'mosher' or whatever people like to call them.** I'm the kinda girl who has chipped black nail varnish smudged black eyeliner wears baggy jeans hooded tops and has very low self-esteem and self-confidence for some reason people have a big problem with me dressing this way. At first it didn't bother me that much but it is starting to really annoy me and sometimes make me depressed and frustrated. The other day some boys put glue all over my coat which was quite new and expensive. There was a girl who tried to help but I didn't even feel I could trust her, 'cos I thought that she was doing it out of pity. 15 year girl.

*Dear 'Non truster'* – You are getting into a really bad situation here where you think that everyone is out to get you. You sound as if you feel self-confident enough to dress differently and be the way that you want to be – and that is great. There will always be someone who will help though – don't lose your trust in people – and it is vital that you accept people's help when it is offered and trust that it is genuine.

# Why people get
# bullied –
# for sex

Many young people can feel pressurized into having
sex, although it is sometimes difficult to know when
pressure turns into actual bullying. It is tricky because
there can be so many conflicting feelings flying
around, but you do need to decide what you want and
what is right for you and stick with your decision. 'No'
should always mean 'No'.

● **SEXUAL TAUNTING**

*Doc* – **I've got a really bad reputation at school for
being easy. All the lasses call me a slag and the lads
call me 'Freddy' and then feel me up.** I've only had sex
a few times and done other stuff. What do I do to get
rid of the reputation? 16 year old girl.

*Dear 'Bad reputation'* – Seventy percent of girls have *not*
had sex by the age of 16, but you need to decide what is right
or wrong for you and stick with it. Let other people know that
whatever they do or say is not going to affect your decisions

48

unless you want it to. This way you will get a reputation for having a mind (and body!) of your own. If you decide that you are going to be 'easy', then you may need to accept your reputation!

## ● DOING THE RIGHT THING

*Dear Doctor Ann.* **I am going out with this boy and I really love him. We both want to have sex but I had a bad past experience and I am worried that he will just use me for sex.** I can trust him but I am paranoid of getting hurt again. 16 year old girl.

**Dear 'Worried about being used'** – The only way that you will not feel 'used' is if you make this decision yourself and don't feel bullied into it. We all learn by the experiences that we have (or should learn) and it is understandable that you are slightly wary of getting hurt again. It sounds as if you are not quite ready for this sexual relationship. Just take it easy, and see how things turn out, and don't let yourself be pressurized.

*Doctor* – **my girl friend and I are going slow at the moment but the other day she said that some friends had been talking to her about how great sex is.** She then asked me to have it with her. I bluntly refused that time and she got upset. Should I have sex with her to keep our relationship going?? 16 year old boy.

**Dear 'Going slow at the moment'** – No, no, no – never have sex just to keep a relationship going. You are doing the right thing in the right way in not allowing yourself to be pushed into something that you (and she) may regret later. Pressure (some of which is bullying) by other people comes in many different forms – and the main thing is to make sure that you make decisions which suit you, rather than other people.

---

*Dear Doctor Ann,* **my boyfriend keeps bullying me into sleeping with him what should I say to him?** 14 year old girl.

*Dear 'Person with a bullying boyfriend'* – You don't want to sleep with this boy, so say NO. If he does not hear the first time say NO again and again until he both hears and believes you. There are lots of other things you can say, like it's illegal, that you are too young, etc., but the main reason is you don't want to and that should be enough. I know it sounds corny, but if he really likes you he won't leave you just because you won't sleep with him.

## ● RESPECTING YOURSELF

*Doctor Ann,* **I've recently started to go out with someone and people are trying to force us to kiss and they're calling me frigid but the only thing is I just feel uncomfortable kissing my girlfriend in front of others.** What's wrong with me?! 15 year old boy.

*Dear 'Being Called Frigid'* — There's absolutely nothing wrong with you. Lots of people only want to show affection in private. These people don't even know what the word 'frigid' means... and it has nothing to do with whether you want to display your feelings in public or not. Ignore them, maybe they are jealous. It's the warmth of feeling that you show to your girlfriend in private that matters. You know how you feel about this girl so don't go being bullied by others. It is your life and the way that you live it is up to you.

---

Dear *Doctor Ann*, **I recently went out with this boy who I've been friends with for a while.** He wanted me to let him finger me but luckily I found a way out for a while. But he wouldn't take 'no' for an answer and kept on pressuring me. So I finished it with him and now he is trying it on with an old mate and he is being a complete arsehole to me. What should I do? 15 year old girl.

> *Dear 'Girl who did absolutely the right thing'* – Boys who are nasty to girls who say no are really weak, sad pathetic characters and should be dumped as fast as possible. You've done just the right thing. He's being a bully because he couldn't get his own way. I only hope your friend is as sensible as you have been. Find someone who respects you and values you for your own views on sex and relationships and forget this loser.

---

Dear *Dr*, **the other day my friend told me that she's a lesbian n that she fancies me n she keeps coming on to me at school n stuff.** I am straight n have a bf and we're perfectly happy with every thing but she's really cumin on strong n i don't like it plz help. 16 year old girl.

> *Dear ' Being hassled by lesbian friend'* – You need to tell your friend that you do not like what she is doing. It sounds as if her behaviour is becoming bullying and it is out of

order. You may have to tell her that unless she stops coming on to you, you will no longer be able to be friends with her. It sounds like she may need to talk to someone else about her feelings. You could suggest she sees the school nurse or counsellor.

# Why people get **bullied – body bits**

In many ways we are all the same – two eyes, one nose etc – but at the same time we are also all different when it comes to the detail! This is all for the good because when it comes to being attractive to, or attracted by, someone else – some like one thing and some another. Alas, this doesn't mean that we are always happy with the way that we are ourselves – but in spite of other people's rude and sometimes hurtful remarks, we have to live with the way that we are.

● **BULLYING ABOUT GIRLS' BITS**

*Dear Ann* – **I have got small boobs and I have started my periods. All my family have got big boobs. Why am I the only one?** All my friends have got big boobs and why do they slag me off about it? 15 year old girl.

*Dear 'Small boobs'* – I get many emails complaining of the opposite – from girls worried about having breasts which are too big. Forget other people's comments. Live with yourself as you are. There is a huge variety of people in the world and they all find different things sexy! Boys love girls with small breasts as well as big ones. Also, remember – just because you have started your periods it doesn't mean that your breasts won't grow bigger over the next few years.

---

*Dear Ann* I'm in year 9 at school and I have developed quite large breasts I'm a C cup. It sometimes gets me down because the girls think that I'm a slag and say that I stick them out but I don't I just can't help it and the boys take advantage of me and think I'm easy when I'm not. They will also frequently grope my breasts which really annoys me. What can I do? please, please help!! 14 year old girl.

*Dear 'Girl with quite large breasts'* – It sounds to me as if your friends are really jealous of you. An awful lot of bullying is really just people being jealous of someone else and feeling rather inadequate themselves. I receive just about as many letters from girls complaining about their breasts being too small as being too big. As for boys 'groping' you – that is totally unacceptable. Remove their straying hands and tell them to keep their hands to themselves or you will go to a teacher.

---

*Dear Doctor* I was bullied and I was every one's main target. The most saddest thing about it was they bullied me because I was flat chested. Bye now doctor Ann. Girl aged 15.

*Dear 'Bullied for being flat chested'* – Your story shows how bullies like to find any excuse to 'get at' others given that we are all 'flat-chested' to start with. Bullies just have to look for something – and will stop at nothing in order to find something which will soothe their own hurt or feelings of inadequacy.

## ● BULLYING ABOUT BOYS' BITS

*Dear Dr Ann* **My balls are really low and I mean really, really, really, really, really, really, really, really, low and my willie is large and all the boys tease me and call me names – wadda I do?** 14 year old boy.

*Dear 'Very, very low balls'* – The making of sperm in your balls is very dependent on temperature. Testes need to be kept at a constant heat. Normally people's balls hang low or high according to the temperature of the air they are in. When it is hot, balls tend to hang low; when it is cooler, they tend to hide away up inside you to stay warm. There is a great deal of variation between boys/men as to what level their balls actually hang (just as there is variation in the size of men's flaccid penises) but they all get lower and larger with puberty. So if everything else is working OK try to ignore the teasing and just be happy that your willie is large (as most boys worry about theirs being small).

*Dear Doctor* – **my best friend has found a lump on one of his testicles. He told his best friend and he spread it round the whole year.** He is really embarrassed and gets teased about it. To make matters worse for him he is convinced he has cancer. Please help. 16 year old boy.

Dear Person 'With a friend with a lump on one of his testicles' – You sound like a really good friend. Instead of teasing your friend about this like other people, you have decided to try and find out more about how to help him. Any lump on the testis needs to be checked out quickly by a doctor. If a lump of the testis is found to be cancer then there is a very good chance that it can be completely cured as long as it is caught early enough. So tell your friend not to delay. However, he doesn't have to panic – there are lots of other more common causes of lumps in the testes which are not so serious – including a hernia, a build-up of fluid called a hydrocele or a build-up of sperm called a spermatocele – all of which can be easily sorted.

## ● SPOTS AND FRECKLES AND MORE

*Dr Ann* **please help me! I have loads of spots and I've been 2 the docs already and nothing works! I'm even getting bullied at school 4 it! i cant take any more HELP!** 15 year old boy.

*Dear 'Person with spots'* – I am so sorry that you are being bullied about this. Just about everyone gets a bit of acne (as this is what your spots probably are) at one time or another, so there is no reason for them to pick on you. Bullies will pick on almost anyone for anything. First deal with the acne itself – get back to your doctor double quick to get something else for the spots. There are loads of treatments and you just want to experiment with different ones, till you find one that works for you. As far as the bullying is concerned – if you really want to turn off the bullies in a big way – the most effective thing to do is ignore them completely. Bullies only get their kicks if they can actually see that they are making someone else feel bad. If you totally ignore them then they have nothing to feed off and will look elsewhere.

*Doctor –* **I have got ginger hair and freckles and everyone takes the micky out of me please help.** 13 year old boy.

*Dear 'Ginger hair and freckles' –* You are not going to change from having ginger hair and freckles so I would suggest that you enjoy the fact that many people find this combination particularly attractive. Ignore those jealous people who want to put you down by 'taking the micky' out of you.

*Dear Doctor Ann –* **what do u do if u get called names coz of wot u look like?** coz I do and it is doing my head in. please help! Thanks from 14 year old girl.

*Dear 'Being called names for what I look like' –* You can try to take no notice of what they say and you can also try telling someone else about what is happening, such as your parents or a teacher. You could also try following advice from people who have been bullied themselves (see chapters 13 and 14 in this book) and found ways of stopping it.

*Dear Doc* — **my hair has grown REALLY BIG!** My mum and dad can't afford to get me a hair cut. I really need to get a hair cut since all my friends at school are beginning to tease me and I don't like it. They call me things like Afro head and I need to do something about it what shall I do? 10 year old boy.

*Dear 'Really big hair'* — It is a strange thing about girls, but many of them love cutting boys' hair. Ask around and I bet a girl out there would be more than willing to do it for you for nothing. You could also check out as to whether one of the local hairdressers has a training night when they do haircuts for free. Anyhow what is wrong with having an Afro haircut?

*Dear Doctor Ann* — **I have been bullied ever since middle school. I have long strawberry blonde hair which goes down past my waist.** This is the main reason people bully me because they are jealous. I am also thin which people see as an opportunity to call me anorexic. I cope with bullying by listening 2 my favourite music at night and doing social things 2 make me feel better! 13 year old girl.

*Dear ' Person with long strawberry blonde hair'* — I am sure that you have analysed your bullies' motives exactly right – they are jealous – so why don't you ignore them and just let them stay being jealous. Don't let them get you down – just carry on doing your own thing and stay the way that you are – brilliant.

*Dear Doc* — **help me please. I get called a man all the time coz I have a really bad deep voice.** Also I have a really big nose and I've got bowed legs and it always looks like I've crapped my self. 15 year old girl.

*Dear 'Getting called a man'* — It seems like someone is just out to get you at the moment because some women have made a fortune out of having a deep voice – though it is usually referred to as being a 'husky' voice. Ignore, ignore, ignore and get on with the more important things in life – though I do realize that being called a 'man' might be seen as one hell of an insult if you aren't one!

---

*Doc* — **I have had 3 teeth removed at the front and I now have 4 teeth missing. There is this evil girl who calls me bugs bunny.** What can I do? 12 year old girl.

*Dear 'Missing teeth'* — The evil girl who is calling you 'Bugs Bunny' must need specs, and you can tell her so. Bugs bunny has two enormous gnashers out front to eat carrots with – not missing teeth. If it is your 'milk' teeth that have been removed – no problem 'cos more will grow. If you have had your permanent teeth removed then your dentist will make you a 'bridge' to fill the gap with artificial teeth. Just try to ignore the bully until time or the dentist have filled the gap.

---

# Why people get
## bullied –
# height and
# weight

You can't choose what height you are, although, to a certain extent, you can do something about your weight! But that doesn't stop people being bullied for being both short or tall, or thin or fat.

● **WRONG WEIGHT**

*Doc* – **some people in my class tease me about my weight but I ask my friends and they say I am not fat why are these people bullying me?** 13 year girl.

> *Dear 'Teased about your weight'* – I am so sorry that you are being teased. No one, whatever their size or shape should get bullied about the way they look. The best thing to do is ignore these stupid taunts. If you really want to find how you compare with others and what is considered normal weight for
>
>  your height – ask your doctor to measure your height and to weigh you and to put these measurements on what is known as a 'percentile' chart. For a 13-

year-old the normal weight range (around their birthday) is between 33 kilograms and 65 kilograms and the normal height range is anywhere between 142 and 169 centimetres. There is an especially wide range of normal height and weight at the time of puberty. Your body is still growing and changing so as long as you are eating healthily and taking exercise you should have nothing to worry about.

*Ann –* **I am totally skinny, and I eat and eat, and just get teased at school 'cos I am like beanpole.** It makes me miserable but I can't seem to do anyfing about it – can u help me? 14 year old boy.

*Dear 'Being teased about being totally skinny' –* The bad thing is that you are getting teased. Actually a great deal of this may be because other people are envious of the fact that you can eat so much and stay thin. The most likely reason that you are staying thin is your genes, which you have inherited from your parents. The main concern of doctors at the moment is about young people being overweight because of lack of exercise and eating too much junk food. If you are eating healthy foods most of the time and doing regular exercise you will end up looking healthy and fit and that is the important thing.

*Dear Dr Ann –* **I am fat and I get bullied a lot at school mainly by the boys and I am very quiet and self conscious and I'm getting myself all depressed and upset about the bullying.** I just don't know what to do. 14 year old girl.

*Dear 'Fat and being bullied' –* This bullying is totally unacceptable. Try not to get depressed by it – especially as people often eat more when they are feeling low. Telling someone, like a good friend, parent, teacher or your doctor, might help as I am sure they would be sympathetic. Meanwhile, if you want to, try and do something about your weight. Don't go on a very strict diet as you probably won't be able to keep this up and then will feel even more depressed if you start putting weight back on again. The easiest way to start is by cutting down on fatty foods like chips, butter and cheese. Try eating more fruit and vegetables (5 portions a day). Don't pile your plate up too high. Start now, and at the same time try taking more exercise – nothing startling – but things like fast walking, cycling, swimming etc. Try taking exercise every day. It is recommended that you should do about 20–30 minutes every day. This exercise will also help drive away your depression.

***

*Dr Ann –* **I am really depressed because I have always wanted to be thin but I am not and people make fun of me for wanting to be thin and I HATE IT.** How do you make them stop? 15 year old girl.

*Dear 'Wanting to be thin'* – Teenage magazines and other fashion magazines tend to have 'stick-like' models – many of whom have eating disorders like anorexia nervosa, and you would not want to be like that. Why not be happy with a normal weight rather than being thin? You say that you are 15, and if you are near your birthday this means that your normal weight can be anywhere from 40–73 kilograms. Your height could be anywhere from 150 cm to 175 centimetres. Bullies tend to pick on people who lack confidence, so if you try to be happier about the way you are then they might leave you alone.

---

*Dear Ann* — **I am a fat, fat man.** Ultimately I can not stop gaining weight and all my mates are taking it out on me. I don't know why. I have a good diet of 2–4 fruits a day, not a lot of bread or pasta, plenty of veggies, and not a lot of red meat. Sweets aren't an issue either. That is only for holidays (but still not that much). I have been fat since like 5th year. I don't want to lose any weight because if i continue to grow in height I will be comfortable. I am currently 5' 11" and 260 lbs. I run a mile 2 times a week and weight lift three times a week, and it is not helping me maintain the same weight. What should I do? 15 year old boy.

*Dear 'Fat, fat man'* — Whether you are fat or not, other people should NOT be teasing you about your weight. Maybe you should get some new friends? But, if the figures you have told me are accurate, I have to agree with you – you are very fat and that is unhealthy. If everything you say about what you eat, and the exercise that you are taking is true – then there is something wrong and you need to see your doctor now. However, it might be that you are kidding yourself about how much you are really eating.

● **WRONG HEIGHT**

*Dear Dr Ann* — **I'm 13 years old and I'm only 4 foot nine inches and every one picks on me.** 13 year old girl.

*Dear '13 year old'* — At 4 ft and 9 inches you are within the normal limits of height for your age. Also, you may not have had your pubertal growth spurt yet – the marked increase in your growth rate that normally happens when you start puberty. That may explain why you are short compared with others around you. Many of them may have gone through their pubertal growth spurt already. The other possibility is that your parents are short, which makes it more likely that you will be short. People who pick on you because of your height are bullies and should be treated like all other bullies – ignore them and if that doesn't work talk to your parents or teachers about it.

---

*Dear Dr. Ann,* **I'm a 17 old Male, nearly 18 at Christmas, I'm 6ft tall and very thin, I'm going to go weight training to help my body fill out.** The problem is, I look very young in the face and my head is small like a child's. Will I fill out in the face and grow? I know this is a strange one for you, but I'm really worried as it makes me feel bad about myself, because all my friends tease me about it. Plz help me. Thanks.

*Dear 'Thin 17 year old'* – I think you are feeling bad about yourself because of your friends teasing you, rather than the shape of your body, which may be like it is in part because of your genes. Weight training will make your muscles grow, and your face may fill out in time. Ignore your friends' teasing if you can or confide about how you feel with someone who is a real friend and doesn't make you feel unhappy about the way you are.

# Why people get bullied – race and culture

All forms of bullying are nasty, but racial bullying is one of the nastiest. People from other countries, other religions and other cultures are easy targets because they have some aspects of themselves which are so obviously 'different' and these 'easy' differences are what bullies love to pick on.

## ● BECAUSE OF THE COLOUR OF YOUR SKIN

*Dear Doctor Ann,* **I am an Asian living in a predominantly English area. I get beaten up and spat at even by people younger than me.** I can't speak to anyone because they wouldn't understand. I feel really down and cry a lot because of it. Who can I tell and what can I do? 15 year old girl.

*Dear 'Person being beaten up and spat on'* – This is racist behaviour and totally out of order. You should tell your parents, teachers, friends – anyone you feel comfortable talking to. You should find that they'll all be sympathetic about this bullying.

Unfortunately, ganging up together against others who are in some way different than themselves seems to make some inadequate people feel good. Try to find a friend who will support you – and go with you when you go out anywhere. It doesn't matter whether they are Asian, white or any one else as long as they are not racist, are against bullying and are on your side. Remember there are lots of people who are very strongly anti-racist and anti-bullying whatever their colour or race.

---

*Dear Doc A,* **at school and on the bus I get made fun of because my skin is very pale white. People call me 'Casper', 'Zombie' and 'Ghost Boy'.** This is making me very depressed. Help?!

> *Dear Person with pale skin* – I'm tempted to say just ignore them, but I know that this by itself may not always make it OK because it is sometimes almost impossible to do. But try not to let them see that you are upset or they will tend to do it more and more. You need to tell someone. Find out what anti-bullying policy you have at school. The best anti-bullying policies in schools are ones that have been discussed with the pupils in the school themselves so that everyone is agreed about what should happen to any bullies.

---

*Dear Doc* – **I get called a 'nigger' because of the colour of my skin so do I have the right 2 beat them up.** Please reply. 14 year old boy.

> *Dear Person 'being bullied because of the colour of skin'* – I sympathize that you feel angry and want revenge against these bullies, but you have no 'right' to beat them up. If you hurt someone through being violent to them physically,

then you can be had up by the police for grievous bodily harm (GBH), just like anyone else. Anyway, beating up the bullies won't solve your problem or make society a better place. It just brings you down to the level of a bully as well. The right way to deal with this is to discuss what is happening to you with your teachers, because your school should have an 'anti-racist' and an 'anti-bullying' policy and there may be other boys or girls who are getting racial abuse. By dealing with this problem through the teachers and the school as a whole, others will benefit as well as yourself.

---

*Dr. Ann.* **I'm in love with a girl and she's in love with me. But she is black and I am white.** My family don't like the fact of my going out with a black girl and are pressuring me to break it off. She's really sweet in many ways. What should I do? 18 year old boy.

*Dear 'In love with a girl who is black'* — At 18 years old it is your choice who you go out with and as you know the colour of a person's skin shouldn't make any difference. But having said that, many people,  particularly of the older generation, still have prejudices that they find difficult to shake off. You are going to need to face up to your parents and not give in to their bullying. If you can talk about this with them in a calm and adult way, in time they should come to understand and respect your feelings.

## BECAUSE OF YOUR CULTURE

*Dear Doctor Ann* — **I am a Jew and my friends make fun of me.** 17 year old boy.

*Dear 'Being made fun of because of being Jewish'* — Making fun of people and deriding them because they are Jewish or of any other religion is totally wrong, though of course it's OK to have arguments and discussions about different religions and cultures! Unfortunately, there has been a long history of antisemitism (being nasty to Jews) in various countries, culminating in the murder of 6 million Jews by the Nazis in the Second World War. Perhaps the bullies are also jealous because Jews have, in many ways, been extremely successful in the world, both historically and today. You say that the people who are teasing you are 'friends'. This must mean that there are some positive things about your relationship with them, so perhaps it is best to just ignore their teasing when it does happen. Either that, or be perfectly frank with them about the way that it makes you feel.

## ● BECAUSE OF YOUR COUNTRY OF ORIGIN

*Ann* — **I live in Spain and I get bullied by the Spanish kids in town sometimes, they call me racist names or say I'm fat, which I'm not.** They also make fun of the fact that I'm British and tell me to go home etc., but this is my home now. They hate foreign people so much that they completely trashed our school (it's an English run international school and we also have a lot of German, Dutch and Norwegian people). My best friend went to the local Spanish school for a year and she had to leave because she got pushed around a lot, beaten up and people stole her things. I try to make sure I'm always with someone else if I'm in town, or avoid the places where they hang out. Girl aged 14.

*Dear 'Bullied in Spain'* — This is no different than the English bullying the Spanish when they come into our schools. Bullies are bullies the world over – always looking for ways to put other people down so that they can feel better about themselves. It has to be the stupidest way for human beings to behave to one another – but we all know that it happens – and sadly you are experiencing it first hand. You just have to make the bullies realize that you have a life of your own and that you are going to live it – whatever they say to you. I am sure that there are some young Spanish people around who would be happy to be your friend – not everyone everywhere is a bully (thank goodness). So ignore the stupid and the weak, and find strong reliable people regardless of the country that they come from to be your friends.

---

*Ann* — **I'm a European in my school but no one else is so I feel left out.** I say 'European' because although I am actually from France, I believe that we all live in a common European community and that being French shouldn't make me any different from being English. 15 year old girl.

*Dear 'European'* — It is so good to hear someone calling themselves 'a European'. Maybe we should take it further and say 'I am a human being' in that we are all basically the same in the world, with the same needs – food, water, shelter, love etc – first and foremost. Try not to feel left out because it is the people who are teasing you about being a 'European' that should feel excluded as they belong to a far, far smaller community of narrow-minded bullies.

---

# Why people bully – through the eyes of the bully

It's hard for most of us to understand why anyone would ever want to bully another person. Some bullies may not always be aware of what they are doing; some are bullying others because they were bullied themselves. In this chapter some bullies give their point of view.

## ● WHEN BULLIES WANT TO STOP

*Doc* – **I have never been bullied but I do bully.** I'm 14 yrs old and myself and 3 other girls bully another girl. We all hang around together, even the girl that we bully, and she is our friend but we are all nasty to her. We pick on her and say nasty things to her. I wish we would stop. We have all tried to be nice to her but we just

can't. We've even tried to get rid of her by falling out with her coz we hate hurting her so we thought she should find new friends but she just cried. So we had to make friends and we're still being nasty to her. Plz help me!!!!!! Girl aged 14.

*Dear 'Bullier'* – What is outstanding here is that you realize what you are doing and can be so open about it. That has to be a beginning. But why do you do it? What kind of satisfaction does it give you? Does it make you feel good and powerful – being able to make someone else miserable? Does it make you feel that you can't be bullied yourself, if you are bullying someone else? You obviously can put yourself in your victim's shoes, so that you understand what it would be like to be bullied. You don't want this, so put an end to it now. Maybe you and your friends should get together and talk to this girl and explain that although you can stay friends, it might be better for her to find some new mates to hang out with who she would get on better with and who would be nicer to her.

## ● BEING BULLIED AND BULLYING BACK

*Dear Doctor Ann* – **I was bullied at school until I started hitting back.** Then I was labelled a bully for sticking up for my self. Boy aged 15.

*Dear 'Bullied turned bully'* – It's understandable that you feel like hitting back, but doing the same thing to other people won't help anyone in the long run. It just perpetuates the bullying within groups of people. Bullying, like parents smacking children, just has to be made totally unacceptable in our society – and the best way of doing that is to have a zero tolerance policy to bullying in all schools.

*Dear Dr Ann.* **I was bullied and it started last year when a boy started coming on to me.** When I didn't respond he called me a lesbian. Then about 2 weeks ago it all finished. As you know its hard to ignore a bully but I did but he started hitting me so I pushed him away and he fell on the floor. I am particularly weak so it damaged his ego and he hasn't said anything since except now he is calling me a bully! 14 year old girl.

**Dear 'Being Bullied and called a lesbian'** – The best way of handling a situation like this is to stay out of the bully's way. Better to stay out of reach than to get into situations where you have to be physical back. If you hit a bully back then there is a danger that you will get labelled as a bully too.

---

Dear Doctor Ann – **I'm getting bullied, cause I used to pick on all the geeks but all my friends turned against me and now I get bullied with the geeks.** 16 year old boy.

**Dear 'Geek bullier'** – This should be a lesson to anyone who bullies anyone – but particularly those who get at people for trying to work hard at school! Why should people be picked on for enjoying their work and doing well at it? Good for you for realising what you had been doing. The question is what should you do now? I suggest that you make friends with the so-called geeks (who you were bullying before) and together stand up to your old friends who have turned round and are bullying you too.

---

# What to do
## when things don't
## work out

It would be a mistake to suggest that there are always easy solutions for all problems in life. Each and every one of us has a responsibility to try to stop bullying from happening, to try to help people when it does happen, and to shout loudly when nothing is being done about it. Sometimes things don't work out straight away – but don't let that stop you from trying again.

● **DON'T GIVE UP – KEEP SHOUTING**

*Ann –* **I've been bullied for a long time, and I still am. I kept my feelings bottled up, and believe me, it doesn't help, it has made my feelings towards myself even worse.** 15 year old boy.

*Dear 'Been bullied for a long time'*
– You are absolutely right. It doesn't help anyone to keep their feelings bottled up. It's much, much better to tell someone about what is happening and to get help NOW. If no one listens the first time, tell someone else and keep on talking about the problem until someone helps you to sort it out.

*Dear Doctor Ann* — **I am being bullied. These people are spreading rumours about me and my school won't do anything about it.** I have told my year head and deputy head but they won't do anything to stop it. Please help me cos i dont know wot to do!!!!!!!! Girl aged 14.

*Dear 'Being bullied and no one doing anything to stop it'* — You must feel very let down – first being bullied and then finding out that no one in the school is doing anything in spite of the fact that you have told them about it. It is worth pointing out that ALL schools are meant to have an anti-bullying policy. I would suggest that you bring your parents in on this and get them to ask the school what their anti-bullying policy is, and why the school is not taking any action over your complaints. If that doesn't work out – or you want to go down another route – you could talk to your family doctor about it and see if they can get the school to take some action. Good luck and do not give up hope please.

*Dear Ann* — **I got bullied at one school so I moved to another.** I thought it was a good idea... but the bullying was worse at my new school I got pushed into lockers, hit over the head with people's bags and one boy pushed me down the stairs. I got money nicked, constantly called names and blamed for things I hadn't done. In the end I couldn't cope anymore and I got really ill with glandular fever and left the school. Boy aged 13.

*Dear 'Bullying and glandular fever sufferer'* – It is, as they say, 'an ill wind that blows nobody good' – sometimes good things result from bad. It's a pity things got so bad that you became ill, but at least changing school gets you away from the bully and this is sometimes the only solution. All schools should have a 'zero tolerance' policy towards bullying – meaning that NO bullying of any kind is allowed. Where these policies have been brought into schools, they have been very successful – particularly where every case of bullying is immediately dealt with on the spot. I hope that when you get back to school again after your glandular fever, you feel confident enough, or your parents support you to feel confident enough, to make sure that the school takes action against your bullies. That is, if you are going back to the same school as the one you left when you had glandular fever.

## ● FORCING ADULTS TO TAKE ACTION

*Dear Doctor Ann,* **I'm a 7th grader at Middle school. My younger sister just started in September and is already having problems with another girl who thinks she is all that and a bag of chips.** She makes me so mad. She hates me and I hate her. Yesterday, this girl got into a fist fight with another 6th grade friend. My sister tried to stop it because she didn't want him to get hurt. She tried to restrain the girl who then punched my sister in the face over 5 times. My sister got blamed for the fight. Then my sister and this girl were walking into the school and she shoved my sister into a friend and her friend was pushed into the lockers. So at lunch, I gathered with 12 friends and talked to her. I said that if she touched my sister again we will be forced to take action in a very painful way. The teachers are useless 'cos they tell me to back off and that the bullying will go away soon, but it keeps getting worse. My dad wants me to stick up for my sister but the teachers want me to stay out of it. But it's our problem, not theirs. What should I do? Should I take care of it myself? Or let them do it? Girl aged 13.

*Dear Person 'Sticking up for her sister'* — You sound like a battler, and that is great, but facing violence with violence doesn't usually work at any level. So you have to find a different and better way of dealing with this situation other than threatening back. Obviously the bullying is not going to go away if you just 'back off'. You are going to have to continue to demand that the adults around you take action. Your dad needs to see the teachers at your school and demand that the bullies are dealt with. That way you will be helping not only your sister, but anyone else who is being bullied as well.

*Dear Ann* — **I always get bullied by kids at school.** I cope with it by fighting with them and hitting them and then I cry at night! 14 year old boy.

*Dear 'Hitting out'* — Fighting is not the answer – you will just get labelled as a bully yourself and that will help no one. Keeping things bottled up and feeling you have to fight this all by yourself, then crying at night is getting you nowhere except into trouble. It would be more effective to start ignoring and avoiding the people who are bullying you. If that doesn't work then get help from an adult.

## TRYING TO FIND ANOTHER SOLUTION

*Dear Doctor Ann.* **I have been getting bullied in school and I can't sleep at night, I have tried telling the teacher but they won't listen,** so I told my parents and they came up the school to sort things out but they still haven't done anything about it, what can I do? 14 year old girl.

*Dear 'Being bullied'* – The school is in the wrong here as they should be taking action to stop all bullying. Don't give up – keep on telling people about it, especially your parents. You are not making an unnecessary fuss. Perhaps you should encourage your parents to go above the school's head to the local education authority if the school doesn't deal with the problem. In the meantime, hang around with a friend who is supportive of you, because bullies prefer to pick on someone when they are by themselves. Try ringing Childline on 0800 1111, which is a free telephone helpline, if you need to talk about this some more.

*Doc* I'm still being bullied at scholl even though the teachers tell my mum thay have sorted it. Boy aged 15.

*Dear 'Don't know what to do'* – Oh, dear – you make me feel bad about being an adult. Teachers are meant to be *'in loco parentis'* which means that they take over the responsibilities of your parents when you are at school. I am sure that your parents would stop anyone from bullying you if this was happening at home – so your teachers should do the same at school. I can see that such a total failure by your

teachers must make you feel very let down. So who else can you turn to for help? Your mum and dad, your family doctor, a close friend within the family – they could all help. They could go to the school and demand to know what the anti-bullying policy is, because each school should have one, and the teachers should be protecting you against this kind of bullying. Take action – keep talking about this until something is done. Another thing you could do is to contact www.bullying.co.uk or look at the bullying section at www.nspcc.org in the kids zone.

# Being bullied?
## things you can do for yourself

To deal with being bullied there are some things which you can try for yourself. Here, people who have been bullied themselves tell us about the tactics they used to stop the bullies. See if they work.

### ● IGNORE THE BULLIES

'When I was bullied I just ignored what everyone said, no matter how hard it was. I let them do it, because all bullies want is a reaction and if they don't get it they stop bullying.' Boy aged 15.

'When I first started at my school, I had loads of 'friends' but after a while they started being nasty. They kept pushing me and tripping me up but the worst of all they  called me names. Sometimes I just cried in my room but I knew I had to do something about it. One day at lunch they decided to do it again but I didn't let them I just ignored them and carried on with my life. A few days later they came up to me and asked to be my friend, I said 'no' and walked off. Now I found some new friends, and the old ones don't come near me anymore.' Girl aged 14.

'I was bullied when I was in year 7 & 8, by this girl and her friends, who would never do anything so big that a teacher would notice, but loads of little things like stealing my friends or leaving me out. I cried heaps, so they slagged me about that too. But after about a year, I realised that the world was a bigger place, and these people didn't really matter about my future. So every time they were horrible, I just ignored them, and thought how much better I was than them. With the help of 2 close friends who stuck by me the whole time, I managed to survive high school!' 14 year old girl.

'Find your own friends and completely ignore anything anyone else says to you – they're not worth your worries.' 16 year old girl.

## ● BE SELF-CONFIDENT

'I always get called names at school, coz I try hard, but I think the best way to get through it is try and be confident in yourself and be thankful 4 who u r, and take no notice of wot others say. Concentrate on the nice things people have 2 say about u, after all that's the only thing that matters!' 14 year old girl.

'I used to get bullied. They would call me lots of names like 'fat' bitch and 'ugly' bitch — it was not nice but then I said to myself 'bullies are cowards'. Don't let them bring you down — just have confidence in yourself. I said that and ignored them and my friends also help me know it is true. Now I don't get bullied any more and I have more friends than ever and I am happy. So any one getting bullied don't let them get ya and don't let them see you are upset about it. That just makes them happy and they will keep at ya. They are cowards and whatever you do don't move school for them because that gives them satisfaction and they will go around saying you moved school because you got bullied and they will be happy and pick on another person.' 15 year old girl.

## ● STICK UP FOR YOURSELF

'I was bullied all through my school years by several groups of girls and it used to get me down in such a way as I wouldn't even go out. But one day I just got sick of it, so I turned round and laughed in the girl's faces and told them I didn't know what sort of a sick sense of humour they had but it wasn't funny and that the only people they were making look bad was themselves. I still don't talk to these girls but at least I don't have no more bother with them. I don't care what teachers and adults say but telling on them only makes it worse. The only way to stop it is to not fight back, but to stand up for urself and show them that u r not afraid. I was petrified of getting beat up but I just pretended to be brave

81

and believe me it worked better than just running to someone else to sort it out for u. Someone who bullies someone else is obviously jealous of that person 'cause they would not be picking on them otherwise. So girls/boys, if u r being bullied stand up for urself cause u r worth more than the bully.'

'When I was bullied I really stuck up for myself and they didn't like it at all. If that doesn't work keep on telling the teachers and they have to do something about it. Or if it is serious go to the head teacher.' 14 year old boy.

'I have managed to survive bullying in a number of ways: 1) Stand up for yourself. Make them feel threatened, but don't lower yourself to their level and start bullying. 2) Ignore them, the bullies only will continue if you don't ignore them. 3) Finally, don't let them get to you. The bullies will taunt you even more if they know they are getting to you.' 14 year old boy.

'Stand up to the bullies. Don't walk past them with your head down and a grim face. Walk past holding your head up high and smiling, be confident. Show them they don't hurt you (even if they do). Don't lower yourself to their level, if they call you don't get mad or call them back just laugh it off and walk away — show them they don't bother you.' Boy aged 15.

**'They r just jealous of u so don't let them get u down. Just laugh at them!!!'** 15 year old girl.

*'I am being bullied at the moment. I usually twist their words round to go against them or turn what they say into a compliment. It works. For instance, if they said 'You're a geek', I'll say, 'I'm a geek and proud of it!' They can't really say anything back to that, well, in my experience! Good luck to all you people.'* Girl aged 16.

## ● SEE THAT YOU ARE BETTER THAN THE BULLIES

**'There were these three girls in my year and I was best friends with one of them and, to cut a very long and painful story short, she just stopped being friends with me. No reason given, she just blocked off. I was in bits and it was my first term in a new school where I knew no one.** She and her two other friends would just talk purposely loud in class about me and no doubt the teachers heard them, but chose to ignore it. I told my mum and she told me to tell a teacher, but I thought if I did that, they'd think I was a goody-goody-two-shoes and ran to the teacher (as they already thought I was a 'nerd') so, it was hard I know. I held my head up high and ignored them, made new friends and basically got over their immature attitude. It hasn't fully stopped (even though it was two years ago) but every time they bad mouth me I just think, nobody in my year likes them, and I have twice as many friends as them. I don't need to get pissed or stoned to have a good time (they began bad benders and hard drugs just after I stopped being friends with them) it was hard, it is hard – but I'm surviving.'

*'I get through by just knowing this — as long as I'm not bullying others, the bullies are lesser humans than me. Anyone who is bullied or doesn't bully anyone else is better than all the bullies in the world put together! This gets me through.'* 15 year old girl.

**'I gave the bullies looks to make them feel stupid. If they said something horrible to me, I would look at them (not say anything) but look at them as if they had the problem and it stopped.'** 14 year old boy.

# Being bullied?
## getting help from others

There is no single, right way to deal with bullying – different things work for different people in different circumstances. This is what some young people, who have been bullied, have to say about getting good help from other people.

- **TELL SOMEONE ELSE ABOUT IT**

'I have been bullied for a long time, and kept it all bottled up inside me. It didn't do me any favours, so talk to someone about it. I have just started to talk to someone, and now I know that things can get better. Don't give up. Let people know how you feel, and start from there.' 15 year old boy.

'I have been bullied many times but the best thing to do is to let someone know. It may be scary coz you think it will make it worse but it really doesn't. Let someone know!! A *problem shared is a problem halved!'* **14 year old girl.**

'**Tell someone that you trust so they can sort it out.'** 15 year old boy.

'*I started a new school two years ago and I didn't really feel comfortable in this new school. I made friends with one girl straight away and she's always been my best mate. Then I met another girl — THE BULLY. We were best friends. Well that's what she thought. I only acted that way 'cos I was sick of her bullying. Finally I had had enough and I kept breaking down. But the more I let my feelings out the better I felt and the stronger I felt. I*

*didn't find it easy talking about it 'cos I had already bottled it up for about 10 months. Talking to someone I trusted helped me through it. My school life now is enjoyable. Telling someone helped me and now that bully has moved to Cornwall. That just proves that bullies aren't so hard or dangerous and deep down their weak and only 'act' rough and tough.'* Girl aged 16.

'If you're bullied, tell someone and get them into trouble for what they've done. You could maybe get them fined or banged up for a few months (if they cause you bodily harm) by calling the police.'
Boy aged 15.

## ● A TRUSTED FRIEND IS A GREAT PLACE TO START

'I was being bullied in year 7 and I dealt with it by telling my best friend and our school nurse. It then got to a teacher and the teacher sat us both down and spoke to us one at time without the other one interrupting and it got sorted because the bully realised what she was doing and she said she wouldn't like it if someone was bullying her that way. Now we are friends and she isn't a bully any more and I'm not being bullied.' 15 year old girl.

'This girl was bullying me after school each day. So I thought I should tell my friend and my friend brought a teacher into the scene and the girl who was bullying me got suspended!'
Girl aged 13.

'The best way to help yourself is to talk to a friend that you trust about how you feel, and what is happening. I know it feels as though no one understands, but believe me, they do, if you trust them, they can help.' Boy aged 14.

'When I was bullied I just told my friends and they took me to the head teacher and they told the teacher so I wouldn't have to do it, and the bullies got into trouble and then they left me alone and probably went off to bully someone else.' Girl aged 13.

## • PARENTS CAN HELP

'I was being bullied and I had to tell somebody, so I told my mum and it helped a lot. The bullying was stopped straight away, so if you are being bullied don't keep it locked up. Tell an adult straight away, they really can help.' 14 year old boy.

'It started at primary school. I was about 6 yrs old and the girls who bullied me were in the year above and I told my mum and my mum got in touch with the head teacher and he sorted it! Every now and again it started and in year six when they had left it was the best year ever! But when I started secondary school they started to bully me again and, like before, I told my mum and then my head of year and my form tutor got involved and it was sorted dead quick! Now I just get on with it and I am not friends with the girls that bullied me.' Girl aged 15.

'I was bullied in primary school from the age of 7 to the age of 10. I was always big for my age but I had lots of friends and so I was happy with myself until a few kids in the year above started saying I was 'fat' and a 'cry baby'. It really upset me and so I became isolated from my friends and just wanted to be alone. I didn't want my friends to see me upset. My mum began to see that something was wrong with me and one day as she took my little sister to nursery school (this was attached to the main school where I went) saw me sitting alone crying. She came into the school and I finally told her what was wrong. She convinced me to go and tell my teacher who was really kind and supportive and she had a quiet word with my bullies. After that they each wrote a letter to me saying sorry and I didn't have any more trouble from them.'

'Hello! When I was at primary school I used to get bullied about my weight. I got laughed at and I used to pretend it didn't get to me. Once I remember them hitting me with their bags saying 'your belly is as big as the sky' and I remember running to my dad crying till I got home. He was very good about it. All weekend I was quizzing myself whether I should tell the teacher or not. Eventually my answer was 'yes' 'cos my Dad told me to and when I told her what happened she told off the two boys and one cried saying he didn't do anything and blamed it on the other boy. Do you know how good I felt? I was so happy I had told her and I recommend all people being bullied should do the same. It wasn't just in this case but lots of other people took the mick. Eventually teachers found out and one helped me. I had meetings with her and I can't believe how kind she was about it.'

## ● TEACHERS CAN BE BRILLIANT

'I told the head teacher and he has spoken 2 the bully about it. He has stopped it now. So tell some 1, it doesn't matter who! They can help u sort it out.' 14 year old boy.

'Yes I have been bullied. Best thing to do is tell someone like a teacher about it. Don't fight back unless you really know you have a good come back. This may get you hit though. So don't do it unless you know you can teach the bully a lesson. Stand your ground – he will back off. If you stand there look him in the eye really look him in the eye he will run.' 15 year old boy.

'Dear Doctor Ann – I was bullied at school. It was so bad that I got really down and stopped eating. The bullying didn't stop so then I started cutting myself. Luckily I knew a teacher who I could trust and told her everything that had gone on and she helped me not only with the bullying but my eating disorder and cutting as well'. 14 year old girl.

## ● THERE IS HELP ONLINE

'Dear Doc. I got, and still am, getting bullied quite badly, but I cope with it as I realised the bullies who taunted me for being skinny/brainy were jealous and the other bullies were just lousy and stupid. It also helped to think there was someone 'out there' (on the web at <there4me.com>) who understands and can help you out. After all my bullying experiences I needed a counsellor – so guess where I went? Yep – right to the above named website. Oh and just for those who are scared to talk out, don't talk about it, Oh no, SHOUT ABOUT IT!!! Make yourself heard and get the support you need!!!'

## ● MOVING SCHOOL

**'I left school 'cause I was being bullied so badly there and went to another one and I am enjoying it better at the new school with lots more friends.'** 15 year old girl.

'I tried to cope by moving to another school and I was happy for a while. But then I started to get bullied there and started home schooling and I'm a lot happier now. My advice is don't let the bullies know they are hurting you cos' that's what I did and it just made things worse.' Girl aged 14.

# Need to find out more?

## Bullying help organizations

### Bullying Online
*www.bullying.co.uk*

A website that gives you lots of tips about how to cope with bullying. Bullying Online also has 50,000 leaflets kindly donated by the Persula Foundation. They include 12 of the most common problems raised by parents and pupils. Email *help@bullying.co.uk* for further details.

Individual leaflets can be downloaded from the website, or you can send a stamped addressed envelope to Bullying Online, 9 Knox Way, Harrogate, N. Yorks, HG1 3JL. The leaflets are free – you only have to pay for postage.

### Anti-Bullying Campaign
185 Tower Bridge Road,
London SE1 2UF
Tel: 020 7378 1446

Gives telephone advice for young people who are being bullied. There are also some websites where you can get help.

## Teenage Health Freak
*The Diary of a Teenage Health Freak*
(3rd edition, OUP 2002)
The book that got it all going. Read the latest version of Pete Payne's celebrated diary in all its gory detail, to find out pretty much all you need to know about your health, your body and how it works (or doesn't – whatever).

*The Diary of the Other Health Freak*
(3rd edition, OUP 2002)
The book that kept it all going. Pete's sister Susie set out to outshine her big brother with a diary of her own, bringing the feminine touch to a huge range of teenage issues – sex, drugs, relationships, the lot.

## Teenage Health Freak websites
*www.teenagehealthfreak.org*
*www.doctorann.org*

Two linked websites for young people. Catch up on the daily diary of Pete Payne, age 15 – still plagued by zits, a dodgy sex life, a pestilent sister. Jump to Doctor Ann's virtual surgery for all you want to know about fatness and farting, sex and stress, drinking and drugs, pimples and periods, hormones and headaches and a million other things.

## Other websites for teenagers
**BBC Kids' health**
*www.bbc.co.uk/health/kids*

**Mind Body Soul**
*www.mindbodysoul.gov.uk*

**Lifebytes**
*www.lifebytes.gov.uk*

**There4me**
*www.there4me.com*

## All your problems
**ChildLine**
Studd Street,
London N1 0QW
Freepost 1111,
London N1 0BR
Tel: 020 7239 1000
Helpline: 0800 1111 (24 hours a day, every day of the year)
Provides a national telephone helpline for children and young people in danger or distress, who want to talk to a trained counsellor. All calls are free and confidential.

## Bullying that is making you depressed
**Samaritans**
If you're being bullied and feel you can't cope any longer and want to speak to someone about it, then contact the Samaritans. You can email them at

*jo@samaritans.org*, phone them on 08457 90 90 90 in the UK and 1850 60 90 90 in the Republic of Ireland, or you can find your nearest branch in your phone book. Visit *www.samaritans.org* for more information.

## If you are ill
**NHS Direct**
Tel: 0845 46 47
*www.nhsdirect.nhs.uk*
Talk to a nurse on the phone about any health problem you are worried about.

## Bullied about sex
**Brook Advisory Service**
Young People's Helpline:
0800 0185 023
*www.brook.org.uk*
User-friendly information service, offering advice on sex and contraception for all young people. Will tell you all about local clinics and send you leaflets even if you are under 16.

**fpa (formerly the Family Planning Association)**
2–12 Pentonville Road,
London N1 9FP
Tel: 020 7837 5432
Helpline: 0845 310 1334
(9 am–7 pm, Mon–Fri)
Gives information on all aspects of contraception and sexual health.

# Index